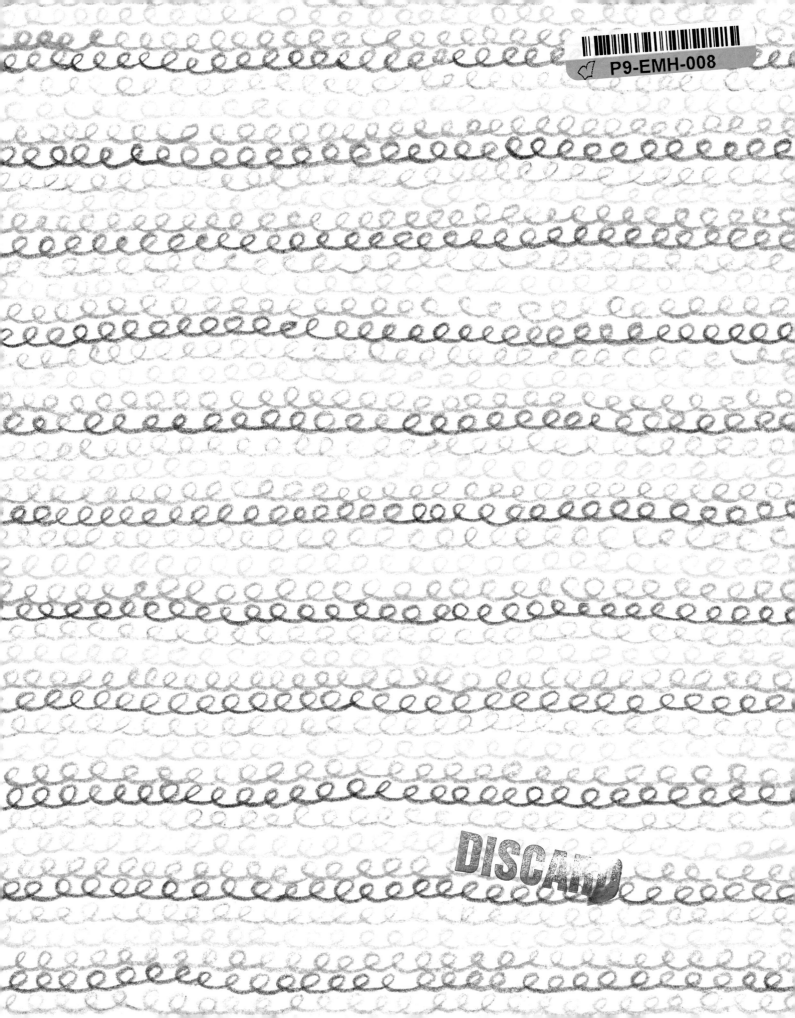

Thank you, Mum and Richard, Sam, James, Ron, and Louise;
thank you also to Jenni Thomas for all her help

Henry Holt and Company, LLC
PUBLISHERS SINCE 1866
175 Fifth Avenue
New York, New York 10010
mackids.com

First published in the United States in 2013 by Henry Holt and Company, LLC.
Originally published in the United Kingdom in 2011 by Macmillan Children's Books.

Library of Congress Cataloging-in-Publication Data
Cobb, Rebecca.
[Missing mummy]
Missing mommy / Rebecca Cobb. — 1st American ed.
p.   cm.
Summary: Daddy comforts and reassures a very young boy after Mommy dies.
ISBN 978-0-8050-9507-4 (hardcover)
1. Death—Fiction. 2. Grief—Fiction. 3. Mothers—Fiction. I. Title.
PZ7.C6338Mis 2013   [E]—dc23   2011052417

First American Edition—2013
Printed in China by Shenzhen Wing King Tong Paper Products Co. Inc.
1 3 5 7 9 10 8 6 4 2

Missing Mommy

Rebecca Cobb

HENRY HOLT AND COMPANY
NEW YORK

Some time ago we said good-bye to Mommy.

I am not sure where she has gone.

I have tried looking for her.

I found lots of her things.

She must have forgotten to take them with her.

We have been leaving her flowers . . .

. . . I don't know why
she hasn't taken them.

I feel so scared
because I don't think she is coming back.

And then I feel angry
because I really want her to come back.

I am worried that she left
because I was naughty sometimes.

The other children have THEIR moms.
It's not fair.

I asked Daddy when Mommy
was coming back.

Daddy gave me a hug
and told me that Mommy had died.

He said that when someone has died
they cannot come back
because their body doesn't work anymore.

Daddy says it was nothing I did
that made Mommy die.

He wishes she was here too, but we are still a family.

I'm glad I have people to care for me.

We can talk about things we remember.

Together we look at pictures
that make us laugh and cry.

And we help each other to try and do all
the things Mommy used to help with.

Daddy says I do them very well.

I really miss my mommy.

But I will always remember her.

I know how special I was to my mommy
and she will always be special to me.

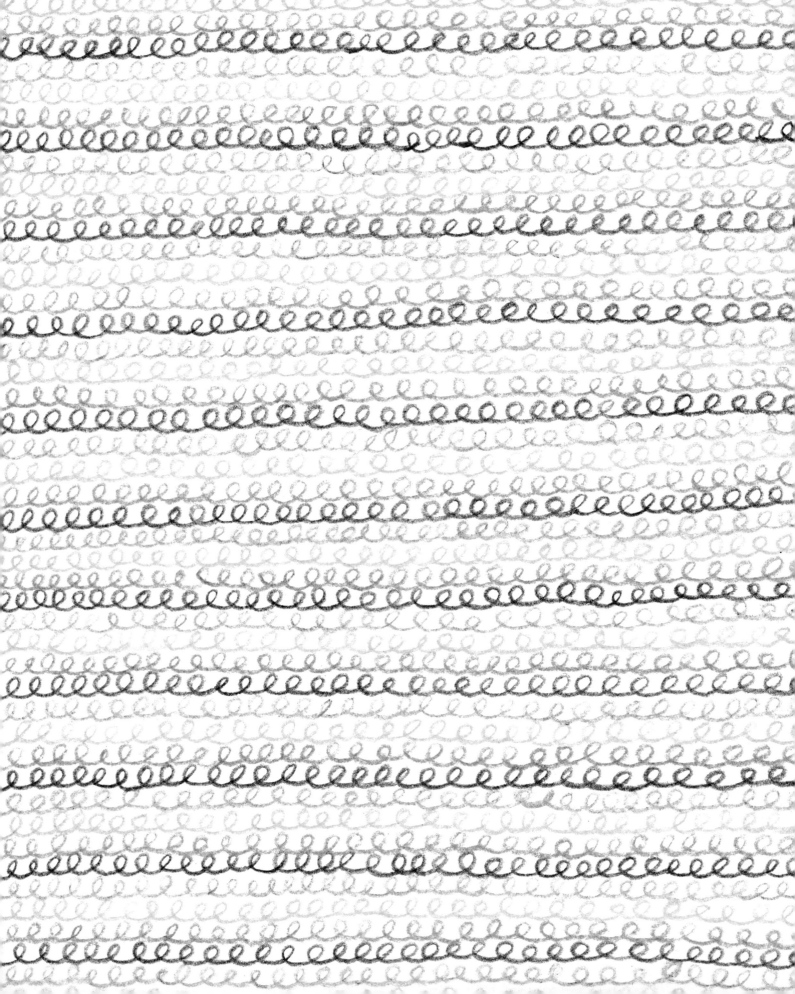